M000020439

# The Power
of the Rose

The Sequel to
*The Haunting of Hawthorne*

by
Anne Schraff

**Perfection Learning Corporation**
Logan, Iowa 51546

Cover Illustration: Mark Bischel
Cover Design: Deborah Lea Bell

**10 PP 08 07 06 05 04 03**

**1** IT MUST HAVE been midnight when the phone rang. I'd only been in bed for about ten minutes. Before that I was on the phone with my friend Dina. We couldn't stop talking about starting college in the fall.

"Oh, my God!" I heard her cry, and I sat straight up in bed. A wave of cold terror washed over me.

I scrambled from bed, not waiting to hear more. I half ran, half stumbled down the hall to my parents' bedroom. "Mom, what is it? What's the matter?" I yelled.

"Your father—" she said to me. My terror grew. I knew he was out there every night driving a cab, and it worried me sick. When he used to be a truck driver, he worked days. But times were hard, especially around here. So he had to take whatever work was available.

"Someone smashed his window with a big rock," Mom said. "Over on Highland, almost right at the Owens' driveway." Mrs.

Owens was my mother's good friend. And her daughter Janessa and I had recently begun hanging out together.

I felt my legs slamming like a jackhammer. "He's okay, isn't he?" I asked, trying to keep the fear out of my voice.

"Yes," Mom said. "He was cut by flying glass and he bumped his head. But Mrs. Owens said he was conscious. She spoke to him briefly before calling me. She doesn't think he's hurt too bad. And the paramedics had arrived and were looking him over."

My brain was spinning. What I'd always feared would happen had finally happened. Some crook had hit Dad's cab. Just the other day Janessa had told me about a lot of ugly things that were happening over in her neighborhood. Like Jim Argus and Dennie Plover stealing from parked cars. Jim and Dennie were troublemakers who almost ruined our senior year at Hawthorne High.

My mother dressed quickly, and I threw on a pair of jeans and a T-shirt. Dad was okay, I kept telling myself. Just a bump on his head and a few cuts. In a couple of minutes we'd be in the emergency room and he'd be cracking jokes and cheering us up.

As I turned to switch off my bedroom light, my eyes fell on my most treasured memento. It didn't seem like much—just a pink rose petal in a covered glass dish. But it had been given to me by the boy who'd loved me in my senior year. And every time I felt sad or scared, I'd look at it and feel better. I never talked about the rose petal to anybody—not even Dina or Janessa. I never talked to them about Basil Harris, either. He'd come to Hawthorne High and brought spirit back to the student body and made our senior year special. He'd left me the pink rose and then vanished. Not long after, the rose had also disappeared. Luckily, though, I still had a small part of the flower as a reminder of Basil and the love I still felt for him.

I touched the glass dish and stared at the rose petal. Then I lifted the cover and took a deep breath. The perfume of the rose was as fresh and intense as when Basil gave it to me. I replaced the lid and turned my thoughts back to my father.

When I was seated in the car with my mother, she asked, "You okay, Valerie?"

"Yeah," I said. I have had epilepsy since I was seven years old. I always take my medication, so I never have seizures. But sometimes Mom still worries about me. Dad never does. Dad thinks I can climb mountains, and I love him for that.

"Why would anybody attack Dad like that?" I asked as we drove toward the hospital.

A look of weary bitterness touched Mom's face. "Seems like things are falling apart everywhere. People getting laid off. Lots of hoods hanging around too. I guess busting up a cab seems like the thing to do."

"Mom! There's Dennie Plover!" I cried as we turned a corner. All the ugly memories from school rushed through my mind. How Dennie and Jim Argus tried to mess up the school as Basil was trying to make it better. As we drove by, Dennie yelled something insulting at me.

"I'm glad you'll be going to college in Iowa," Mom said. "Thank God you got that scholarship. You'll be out of all this."

Yeah, I thought to myself, and you and Dad are stuck here! All of a sudden my September journey to that nice college in the Midwest felt like a betrayal.

"Hey," Dad called out to us when we finally entered the emergency room. "I don't feel as bad as I look, so take it easy." He was lying on a cot, his head bandaged, abrasions on his face.

"We were so worried," Mom said. "Lily Owens called and told us what happened. But she didn't see who did it."

"I'm afraid I can't help there either. I didn't see the thing coming. I was going to pick up a fare at the Blackburn Inn—some guy too drunk to drive. All of a sudden my side window comes crashing in and I got a piece of sidewalk in my lap. But I'll be okay. I'll be fine. It's part of being a cabbie in this city, I guess. Goes with the territory."

I hugged my father, trying not to let the tears overflow. He was such a good man. He'd done everything right. Graduated from high school, worked his heart out on the job, put his family first. Now here he was, fifty-four and driving a cab on these mean streets. It just didn't seem fair.

Dad ended up staying in the hospital for two days. He had a mild concussion, and the doctors wanted to keep him for observation. Dad kept joking and saying the nurses were keeping him longer than they had to because he was such a hunk. But when he thought we weren't looking, I saw his hands tremble. I could see the attack had damaged more than his head. He was scared to death. How could he go back to driving a cab?

I couldn't get my dad off my mind. I was still depressed when I went to work on Sunday. I worked part-time at a bagel and doughnut shop to earn money for college expenses not covered by the scholarship.

"Hey, Valerie, indulge me. One fudge doughnut with a deadly dose of chocolate," came a vaguely familiar voice.

I looked up to see Gil Sheffield standing at the counter. Gil had been a football star at Hawthorne. I'd never had much to do with him. But now I noticed that he had a grin that could light up a stadium. "Hi, Gil. I haven't seen you in a while," I said.

"Yeah, Valerie. I've been working a lot of hours at Sal's gas station. I figure I'll work this doughnut off by quitting time."

I scooped a doughnut into a bag and gave it to Gil. "So whatcha doing in the fall?" Gil asked. "Going off to some high-powered college, I bet."

"I planned to go to the University of Iowa, but now I'm not so sure," I replied. I looked around to see if my boss, Mrs. Dowd, was listening. I hadn't shared anything with her about what happened to my dad. She and her twenty-year-old son Rick never seemed much interested in the people who worked for them. Rick and his mother were pretty grouchy people. They were always bickering.

"Hard to leave old friends?" Gil asked. I nodded rather than try to explain.

"Hey, speaking of old friends," Gil said, leaning on the counter and grinning. "You ever hear from that guy Basil Harris? You two were pretty tight at school."

"No. He uh...went back to where he came from," I said.

"Know what?" Gil said, still smiling. "Some guys said Basil was a ghost. I'm not buying that, but he was a little strange." Gil shook his head. "Man, the way he came and turned our school around. It was amazing."

Gil laughed. "There was even a story going around school that he was the guy whose statue stands at Hawthorne—old William Evans Hawthorne. You know, back from the dead to save Hawthorne again. Just like he did back in the 1800s when he saved all the students in that big fire. What do *you* think, Valerie? Was Basil a ghost, or what?"

It felt strange to hear Gil put it that way. Basil had flickered in and out of my life— like a ghost. But his kiss had been real. And it was as alive in my memory as the petal from the rose he gave me.

I gave a little laugh. "Is all this leading up to some joke about school spirit, Gil?" I asked. He chuckled, and before he could reply, I changed the subject. "So, where are you going to college?"

"The local junior college. Didn't get a football scholarship like I'd hoped. So I gotta go where the tuition is low," Gil said.

"I uh...might not go to Iowa, either," I said.

"Hey, something wrong?" Gil asked,

looking concerned.

"Well...the other night some creep smashed my dad's cab window. Now he's in the hospital," I said.

"Hey, that's too bad. He gonna be okay?" Gil's big brown eyes filled with sympathy. I felt a little bit ashamed for thinking he was some unfeeling clod just because he played football.

"I guess he'll be okay," I said. "But I don't want him driving a cab anymore. It's too dangerous. I've got a scholarship, but there're still other expenses. I kinda think it'd be better if I hung around here and helped the family. Maybe I could go to the junior college for a couple of years and then transfer to Iowa."

I stopped, surprised at myself for sharing so much with Gil Sheffield. He was almost a perfect stranger. I think in all the time I went to Hawthorne, I spoke to him maybe once. And that was when he was at home with a sore foot. I'd made a copy of some class notes for him and he thanked me a lot.

"That's a tough decision," Gil replied. "But I figure whether you stay or go, you'll do just fine."

At that moment, the front door opened and in came Dennie Plover and his punk brother Keith. Keith stood back with a sullen look on his face. But Dennie came right up to the counter and smirked at me. "Word on the street is that your old man got his head busted, Valerie." He laughed wickedly.

As I glared at Dennie, I felt a terrible rush of hatred. Dennie must not have an ounce of empathy in his body. In fact, I wondered if he had even one positive trait.

I couldn't help recalling how Basil seemed to have this strange power to make awful things happen to bad people. Like the time Jan Draper tormented Mrs. Gottsman, one of the teachers. Basil had simply stared at Jan, and she suddenly felt like mice were crawling all over her.

I wished with all my heart that I had such power right now. I wished I could make something horrifying happen to Dennie Plover right now to wipe that evil grin off his face. A deluge of cockroaches maybe.

The Plovers bought two doughnuts and

then, of course, complained that they were lousy. Rick Dowd gave them another two, free of charge. But even as he apologized, I could see how Rick simmered underneath his fake smile. He seemed to dislike the Plovers as much as I did. But then Rick Dowd sometimes seemed to hate the whole world.

Keith and Dennie soon swaggered out. I glowered after them, wishing a cement truck would hit them.

Only seconds later, I heard brakes scream.

**2** I ALMOST CRASHED into Gil as I raced to the street, dreading to see the Plovers under a cement truck—my hateful wish come true. Instead I saw the two of them parading across the street. A motorist was yelling after them, "Why don't you idiots watch where you're goin'? I almost hit you!" Dennie turned and cursed the driver before he and his brother continued across the street.

"They think they're indestructible," Gil said, shaking his head. "I thought I was too, until I busted my foot and found out there was no football career in my future."

I'd forgotten the consequences of Gil's sore foot until he reminded me. "I'm sorry, Gil," I said sympathetically. "Well, it was nice seeing you again." I turned to go back into the doughnut shop.

"Yeah. Hey, listen, maybe we can get together sometime...." Gil said.

"Maybe," I answered. But my mind

wasn't on Gil. I was thinking about Basil Harris and how great it'd be if he came in about now, wearing his faded jeans and work shirt. I closed my eyes and stepped back into my memories. I remembered him so well—his gentle voice, steady gaze, and his sweet, old-fashioned manners.

But like Gil, I scarcely knew what to call Basil, even now. Once I asked him, "Just who are you, Basil?"

But he never answered me.

\* \* \*

That afternoon Dad came home from the hospital. When we hovered over him, he laughed. "I'll be good as new in a few days," he said cheerfully. Yet I saw that as Mom poured him a cup of coffee, he used both hands to keep the cup from shaking. Still, the coffee almost spilled over the brim.

My eyes filled with tears and I escaped to my room. I didn't want him to see me cry for him. He was so proud, so determined to make the best of everything. He'd feel worse than ever if he thought he was dragging me down.

I pulled out all the material related to

the University of Iowa—the campus map, the class offerings, a student handbook. It became unreal, like reading about a new housing development on the moon. I knew in my heart I wouldn't be going. I couldn't. I also knew there'd be a big fight if I told my parents I was skipping Iowa because of Dad. So I had to come up with another story to convince them.

I walked over to the rose and touched the glass dish. The strange, sweet, unwilted rose was all I had left of Basil. And while I stared at it, an idea came to me. Gil Sheffield wanted to date me. I could tell by the way his eyes sparkled when he grinned at me. I could begin dating him and tell my parents I liked him so much, I wanted to stay here and go to the J.C. too.

I called Dina and told her what I had in mind. Dina was my best and oldest friend. She was always there when I needed an open ear.

"You mean you're going to *just use Gil? Simply pretend to like him?*" Dina demanded.

"*I do like him.* What's not to like about him?" I said evasively. "Maybe I'll grow to like him even more."

"What if Basil comes back?" Dina asked.

I remembered the last time I saw Basil. He had pulled me into his arms and kissed me so sweetly. And somehow I had known that that was the last time I'd see him. So I told Dina just that: "Basil isn't coming back. And besides, Dina, you've been after me for weeks to start seeing other guys. Why the sudden change of heart?"

"I didn't have a change of heart," Dina replied. "I've always thought it's a great idea to go out with someone—if you like him."

Dina was right, I knew. But I couldn't come up with any other plan.

That afternoon I walked over to Sal's gas station and found Gil tuning up an engine. When he sort of flirted with me, I flirted back.

Finally he glanced at the clock. "I'm off in ten minutes," he said casually. "Want to go for a cool drink?"

"Sure," I said. "It's such a hot day."

A short time later we hopped in Gil's old Chevy and drove over to a fifties-style diner. I savored my soda and tried not to think about how I was misleading Gil.

"Your dad feeling better?" he asked me.

"Yeah, he is. But I can tell he dreads going back to driving the cab. The police said the guy who busted his window wasn't just a vandal. He tries to disorient the drivers in order to rob them—and sometimes the passengers. And he carries a gun. See, my dad was slowing for a light. The only reason the guy fled was that a couple of people came running. Dad could've been shot!" I felt my throat tighten again as I pushed away the thought.

"That's rough. Can't he do some other kind of work?" Gil asked.

"Yeah—if he only had time to look for something else. But there are the house payments and all the rest of the bills. And Mom's job as school secretary doesn't pay very well. That's why I'm going to keep on working and go to the J.C. like you. I figure college will be a whole lot cheaper, and I can work too."

"Your dad is gonna feel bad that he's spoiling your plans, won't he?" Gil asked.

Looking into Gil's clear, honest eyes, I

just couldn't deceive him. I took a deep breath and said, "Uh...Gil, I've got a confession to make. And a favor to ask. I'm telling my dad I'm changing my plans because of us," I said.

"Us? You mean you and me?" Gil looked confused for a minute; then he grinned. "You mean you're telling him that we're really serious?"

"Yeah." By now I was so ashamed of myself that I couldn't look Gil in the eye. "I guess I'm sort of using you, huh? I'm sorry, Gil. I've twisted my brain into a pretzel figuring out a better excuse. But right now...."

"Hey, don't sweat it." said Gil. "Once you get to know the great Gil Sheffield, you'll understand what his legion of fans have seen for years." He flashed a smile that could have lit up the whole town.

"I think I already do, Gil," I said with a smile in return. I was relieved Gil had so generously agreed to play along.

Now I just had to get myself ready for confronting my parents. My mom and dad aren't easy to fool. Convincing them I was into a real serious relationship with Gil would be harder than passing the most difficult exam I'd ever taken.

At dinner that night, Dad announced that his boss at the cab company had asked Dad when he would be returning to work.

Her eyes full of concern, Mom asked, "So what did you say?"

Dad shrugged. "I told him time's a-wasting. The unpaid bills are piling up."

"I've almost got the plane fare for Val's trip to Iowa, so there's no need to worry about that," Mom said. I noticed she had big, dark circles under her eyes. I knew she was worried about Dad's safety. "Maybe if you took a few days to look for another job.." her voice trailed off.

"Time is money," Dad said.

"Uh...you guys, I've got something to tell you," I said, my heart pounding. "I'm not going to Iowa for college. I'm going to the J.C."

Dad stared at me in shock. "What on earth—what...I don't understand! Ever since you received that scholarship, going to Iowa has been the only thing on your mind."

"Well, now I've got something else on my mind," I said. "Or, rather, someone. There's a guy I like. Gil Sheffield. He used to play football at Hawthorne, and he's a really nice guy. He's going to the J.C., and I want to spend my freshman year there too. Maybe even my sophomore year."

"Valerie," Mom said with a frown, "it's not like you to let a crush on a boy change important plans you've made. Are you really serious?"

I'd hardly ever fought with my parents. Dina fights with her mom, and Janessa sometimes quarrels with her folks. They sometimes can't believe I'm for real because of how I always get along at home. They tease me about it, but I don't mind. It's just that my parents and I have never really disagreed on a major issue before.

But now I could tell my parents were about to get upset. So I tried to act like Dina does when her mother is on her case over some curfew thing. "I'm eighteen-years old, Mom. I need to have some fun. My whole senior year I studied like mad so I could graduate with honors. And I did. Well, I'm worn out now. I want to have some fun as a freshman at the J.C. I want to kick back, Mom. I can always pick up a scholarship later on for my junior and senior years."

"But, Valerie," my mother said, "you never even talked about Gil Sheffield all the years you went to Hawthorne. You used to make fun of the jocks, remember? And you haven't even mentioned him to us this summer. When did all this happen?"

"Mom," I said, "I admit that I cared so much for Basil Harris in my senior year that I couldn't think of anybody else. And I was wrong about jocks. Now that I'm getting to know Gil, he's really nice. Yeah, I guess it happened kind of sudden. But sometimes it works that way." I could tell my parents weren't buying it. Heck, I wasn't even convincing myself.

After a long silence, my father finally cleared his throat. "Valerie, look me in the eye," he said seriously. "Now tell me you're not doing this because of that stupid thing that happened to me. Because if you are, forget it. I'm not letting what some lousy crook did ruin my daughter's whole future!"

"That has nothing to do with my decision," I quickly insisted. "I want to stay around here and see more of Gil. I want to enjoy some things I never had time for in high school."

"But, Valerie," my mother began, but I interrupted.

"Look, Mom, I want to go to school with Gil, that's all. I spent four years at Hawthorne battling for the top score in every test. Right now I just want to enjoy myself. If I went to Iowa, it'd be big competition all over again."

We finished dinner in strained silence.

Later that night I was sitting in the living room with my father. "Say, Dad," I said. "You won't have to go back to being a cabbie right away, will you? You can wait a little while for something better, can't you? Mom can use the money she's been saving for my plane fare to pay the bills for a month. Maybe you can find something in sales. You know you have the gift of gab, but you've never tried sales."

My father looked off into the distance and said nothing. I tried to fill the awkward silence. "I'm really glad I won't be

going away to college. I would have
missed you guys."

My father stared down at his folded
hands. "Valerie, you know your mom and I
just want what's best for you."

"I know." I managed to keep my voice
steady. But I didn't feel I could keep up
the pretense much longer. As soon as I
could, I slipped away and went outside.

The night was carrying in a cool air, and
twilight brought its usual peace to the
neighborhood. I glanced down the street
and took stock of things.

It really wasn't a bad street. Sure, the
houses were small. But they were well
kept up. People mowed their lawns and
planted flowers. Before I was born, most
of the people who lived here were
German or Irish or English, with a few
Italians sprinkled in. At this point most of
our neighbors were African-American,
Hispanic, and Vietnamese, though some
elderly Germans and Irish remained. We
all got along pretty well.

But a couple of blocks down stood the
projects. An ocean of life crammed into a
couple of acres of buildings. And as in

most oceans, there were the predators. The sharks of the projects, like the Plovers, terrorized the rest. Or perhaps worse yet, they drove the decent people to give up hope.

I heard the wind gently rustling through the old mulberry tree. And then I heard something else. I heard my father crying.

**3** I KNEW MY dad was ashamed that he hadn't done better for us. My father served in the army and was a good soldier. He was *always* a good soldier, even when he became a civilian. He worked hard, he was never late to work, never goofed off on the job.

Then the company he'd given most of his life to got hit by the recession. Dad was one of the unlucky ones to lose his job. He'd tried hard to find another good job, but he couldn't. Maybe it was his age. We could never figure out why no one would hire him.

Dad always did his best for his family, his employer, his country. But the breaks didn't come his way. I guess the breaks don't come a lot of people's way. There are more losers than winners in every game.

Now I wanted to go to my father, put my arms around him, and tell him how much I loved and admired him. I wanted to tell him that no matter where I went to school, I'd make myself a wonderful future. But I knew it'd hurt him even more to realize I'd heard him crying. So I quietly went back into the house.

Sleep didn't come easily that night. I sat in my room looking at my rose petal. And in the middle of my whirlwind of thoughts, I remembered Basil saying, "Few people in this world really care about others. The few who do care make up for all those who don't. You're needed, Valerie. So don't ever lose heart."

"I won't," I whispered to him, wherever he was.

* * *

On Sunday I went to the beach with Gil. Janessa and her friend Tom went with us. It would have been a really fun day if we hadn't run across Jim Argus at the diner.

Jim sauntered over and leaned on top of Gil's Chevy. "Hey Gil—you going out with Valerie now?" he sneered.

"So what's it to you, man?" Gil asked in an annoyed voice.

"Don't you know she has seizures, man? Like a mad dog," Jim said.

"Get lost, Argus," Gil snapped. "Your face is spoiling the looks of the hood."

To Gil's credit as a gentleman, he didn't ask me for an explanation. But I gave him one anyway. Only my closest friends knew about my epilepsy. Jim Argus certainly didn't qualify in that category. However, he'd overheard my speech teacher, Ms. Brundage, gabbing about it with another teacher. I still think it was Ms. Brundage who cheated me out of the chance to be the school valedictorian. She just wasn't intelligent enough to know my epilepsy was completely under control.

After Tom and Janessa took off, I made my explanation to Gil. "One day when I was in the second grade I fainted," I began. "After a lot of medical tests I was finally diagnosed with epilepsy. The doctors gave me regular medication, and it hasn't ever given me a problem. But that doesn't matter to people like Jim Argus. He has a grudge against me because I helped Basil Harris kick him out of the student government. Anyway, I have epilepsy, but it's not a problem for me. Is it for you, Gil?" I said.

Gil smiled and gently shook his head. "Of course not. Besides, I've got my own problems, like dyslexia. I have a terrible time reading."

"Woodrow Wilson had that," I said, "and it didn't stop him from becoming president of the United States."

Gil dropped me off at my door, and we planned another beach date for the next weekend. I told him I really had fun. I was surprised that it was the truth.

But the next day at the doughnut shop, Jim Argus reappeared. "I hope I didn't spoil things with your new boyfriend, Valerie," Jim taunted me. "You know, like you spoiled things for me at Hawthorne. Thanks to you and Harris, my whole senior year was ruined. My parents never got off my case for getting kicked out of office."

"You were a rotten class president," I snapped. "Instead of trying to make things better, you actually encouraged people to make them worse. Whenever somebody slopped graffiti on the walls, you just laughed. When some stupid jerk disrupted a class, you'd join in. You didn't deserve to be student body president."

"So you elected yourself God and decided to trash my life," Jim said bitterly. "And to turn Hawthorne into Geek City. How many brownie points did you rack up for that?"

"Sorry I spoiled your party," I shot back.

"I don't think you realize how sorry you're gonna be," he declared, his eyes glowing with fury.

"Look, I'm working here," I said. "Why don't you go practice your threats in front of the mirror and get them right?"

Jim glared back. "You won't even see it coming next time," he warned. "Just like your old man."

An icy shock ran down my back. Could Jim Argus be the guy who'd been hitting the cabs?

I thought it over and decided he probably wasn't. He was a troublemaker and a punk, but he was as yellow as egg yolk. He wouldn't have the guts to attack cabs. He always followed other punks in their schemes at school, but he never started anything on his own.

More likely it was Dennie Plover or his brother Keith who'd hit Dad's cab. I remember a day not too long ago when they'd tried to attack Basil and beat him with tire chains. They were dangerous and violent. And I'd seen Dennie lurking very near where Dad was attacked as Mom and I drove to the hospital.

When Dina came into the doughnut shop later that day, I shared my suspicions with her.

"I don't think so," Dina said. "I know the Plovers steal out of parked cars and stuff, but armed robbery? I can't see them doing that. Besides, how could you prove it? The cops said the guy always wears a ski mask, so nobody has seen his face."

"Yeah, my dad didn't see a thing," I said.

"Mrs. Owens said she saw the guy sprinting between the buildings after your dad's cab was hit," Dina said. "He always gets away on foot. That's why he's so hard to nail. It's lots easier for the cops to chase a car than a guy who knows all the rat holes to hide in."

Dina studied me for a moment, then asked, "Did your parents buy the stuff about you and Gil being involved?"

"I don't think so, but they didn't fight me.

I kinda think Mom was relieved, even though she wouldn't admit it. She's terrified of Dad going back to driving a cab," I said.

"Well, how was your date with Gil on Sunday?" Dina asked.

"I had a great time," I said. "We're going out again next weekend."

"So, did Gil kiss you?" Dina asked slyly.

"No. I like Gil, Dina. But...." I ended with a sigh. I remembered the first time Basil had kissed me. It was after the school dance, and he'd walked me to the door of my house and asked if he could kiss me. That he should ask and not just do it had seemed so quaint and old-fashioned. His kiss made me feel so magical. I wondered if anybody in the world could ever make me feel that way again.

"You'll get old real fast if you're set on waiting for Mr. Right," Dina said as if she were reading my mind. "There are about fifty wonderful men in the entire world and there are millions of us, right? So only a tiny fraction of us will ever get one of those wonderful guys. The rest of us have to settle for dregs."

"Dregs?" I gasped. Then I laughed.

"Dregs?"

"Sure. Dregs, like what's left in the coffee pot when all the good coffee is gone. Look at me. I'm going with Wallie Sunders. Wallie is a dreg—ask anybody. But if I didn't go with him, who would I go with?" Dina said.

"Oh, come on, Dina. There are plenty of wonderful guys. Gil is definitely *not* a dreg," I said.

"Dream on, girl," Dina laughed.

My conversation with Dina chased Jim Argus' threat right out of my head. But I soon had reason to remember it. Next day at work, when it was almost time for me to go home, Mrs. Dowd said she wanted to see me. "I need to talk to you in the back."

Mrs. Dowd wasn't free with compliments. But she'd told me several times that I was the best counter clerk she'd ever had. I was fast and efficient, and I always worked my full shift. So I wondered what she wanted to see me about.

We went back to the storage room. Mrs. Dowd shut the door and turned to me. "I always thought I could trust you, Valerie. But I realize now that I was wrong. Valerie, you can either quit or I'll have to fire you. I won't have a thief working for me."

# 4

"A THIEF! MRS. Dowd, what are you talking about?"

Mrs. Dowd frowned. "For some time now, cash has been missing from the register each day. I've been trying to identify the person who's responsible. But until today, I wasn't sure."

"I have never stolen from you—or anyone else in my life!" I realized I was shouting, but I couldn't hold in my anger. "Why are you accusing me?"

"Your old boyfriend called me today," Mrs. Dowd began.

"My old boyfriend? Who are you talking about?" I demanded.

"Jim Argus," Mrs. Dowd announced.

The name was explanation enough. Jim had launched his second attack against me.

"Look, Mrs. Dowd, Jim Argus was never my boyfriend. In fact, we've always disliked each other a lot. He's trying to get back at me for helping to dump him out of office at school. Anything he's said about me is bound to be a lie."

Mrs. Dowd shook her head. "The facts are that somebody has been stealing from me and that this Jim Argus said you actually showed him money you'd taken from my register."

"Call the police," I demanded. "Ask them what kind of record Jim Argus has. Then decide whether to believe him or me."

Mrs. Dowd studied me coldly. "Do you really want me to bring the police into this? With the problems your father has had lately, I didn't think you'd want to stir up more trouble."

It was as though a huge wave had smashed me to the ground. My anger was doused, and replaced by a feeling of helplessness and frustration.

Mrs. Dowd sensed the change in me. "I'd prefer to settle this quietly. But if you insist, I'll bring the police in."

I met her eyes and spoke as calmly as I could. "I'm not your thief, Mrs. Dowd. But you're right, my parents don't need any more trouble right now. I quit."

I grabbed my purse and charged out. I

was so furious, I didn't see Gil until he gripped my arm.

"Hey, Val, what's up?" he asked. "You off work early?"

"No. I just got fired. And for the stupidest reason in the world!" I yelled.

"My God, I'm sorry. Come on. I'll drive you home and you can tell me about it," Gil said. It was a relief to have a sympathetic ear. I told Gil everything, including what Jim did.

"Man, what a creep," Gil said. "I remember what a loser he was at Hawthorne. He did a pretty good job of messing up the school—until your friend Harris turned up."

I sighed. "You know, Basil gave me hope that decent people could make a difference. He actually made me believe in justice, corny as that sounds."

"It's not corny. And maybe this is just coincidence, not justice, but I may be able to solve one problem."

"What do you mean?"

"A job. Margo, the cashier at the station, quit last week. Sal is looking for somebody to take her place. And I bet you'll even earn more money. Sal pays well."

"Gil, that'd be great," I said.

Gil grinned. "And don't worry about Argus. I'm gonna have a little talk with him."

"No, Gil, please. The last thing I want to do is start a war."

"There won't be any war," Gil scoffed. "The battle will be over before it's fought."

Before he dropped me off, I kissed Gil. It wasn't like kissing Basil, but it wasn't bad, either.

That evening I told my parents the news—or at least part of the news. "I won't be working at the doughnut shop anymore. I got a better job at the gas station, and I'll be making more money."

"Pumping gas?" Mom asked.

"No, taking money and credit cards. Though I wouldn't mind pumping gas once in a while too," I said.

My father smiled at me. "I don't think there's much you couldn't do if you put your mind to it," he said with pride.

The next day I talked to Sal, the gas station owner. To my relief, he didn't call Mrs. Dowd. Before the morning was out,

I'd started my new job. Once I learned how to work the little computer, it was a lot easier than working at the doughnut shop. And I liked the extra $1.50 an hour.

I also liked Sal. He was a big, burly guy with an explosive laugh. About seven years ago he'd come to the United States from Colombia. After a lot of hard work, he'd put enough money aside to buy this station. I respected Sal for that. And he was a lot more fun to work with than Mrs. Dowd and her grouchy son.

Early in the afternoon Rick Dowd came in to pay me for gas he'd pumped. "Hey, you working here now?" he asked me.

"Yeah," I said. I felt like telling him what a rotten thing his mother had done to me, but he beat me to it.

"Me and my mother had a big fight over firing you. If she'd bothered to ask me, I could have told her that Argus was a liar. Leave it to her to make a stupid move like that. But you're better off outta that dump. I'm taking off myself pretty soon, when I got enough money," Rick said.

I took Rick's cash and he gave me three bucks for a tip. When my eyes widened in amazement, he said, "I'm not cheap like my old lady."

My first day at the station went by very quickly. After work I went out for pizza with Gil. I was beginning to really enjoy hanging out with him. He listened to what I said, shared a lot of my interests, and was just plain fun to be with. I didn't feel anything special toward him yet—no more than you'd feel for a favorite cousin or something. I hoped that was all it was with him too. I didn't want him to end up getting hurt.

Over our pizza Gil said, "I had me a little chat with Jim Argus. I don't think he'll bother you again."

I looked up sharply. "You didn't do anything stupid, did you?"

"Like busting him in the face?" Gil asked, chuckling. "Not my style. I'm a gentle giant. But when a six-foot-two-inch dude like me looks down at a five-foot-seven-inch dude like him, I get a lot of respect for what I'm saying."

When Gil dropped me off at home, my dad was waiting for me with a big smile on his face. "Guess what, honey? I got a job!" he announced.

"Dad, that's wonderful! What kind of job?" I asked. I hoped he wasn't going to say he was driving for another cab company. Since his attack, another cabbie had been attacked on Brewster Street—and he'd almost lost an eye. His passenger, an elderly woman, was robbed too. But from the look on Dad's face, I didn't think it was another cab job.

"I'm going to be selling cars," Dad crowed. "I'm really excited about it. I can make some real money if I get to be good at it."

I hugged my dad. "That's fantastic!! And I know you'll be great. You could sell air conditioners in Greenland in the middle of winter!"

Dinner was nice that night. I liked my new job, and Dad was optimistic about his. That made Mom happy. I was also looking forward to going to the beach with Gil that weekend, especially since we were going with Janessa and Dina and their boyfriends. Having all of us together was three times as much fun.

Then, around 7:30, Janessa called. "I

saw Jim Argus this afternoon and was he weird!" she said.

"What do you mean, weird?" I asked.

"Like, I started razzing him about messing with you and making trouble at your job. Suddenly he gets this strange look on his face and mumbles something about how he's never gonna bother you again," Janessa said.

"Uh...Gil sorta talked to him. Maybe Jim's scared of him," I said.

Janessa laughed. "Our Gil? No way, girl. He thinks he's a big tough dude when he talks in that rumbling voice and tries to act mean. But everybody can see he's a pussycat."

"Then what got Jim so spooked?" I asked.

"Get this: He thinks you've got some supernatural power!" Janessa giggled.

"Supernatural power?" I gasped.

"Yeah. He says you're as strange as Basil Harris was. Remember how kids said he could look at somebody and make things happen? Like when Dennie said Basil looked at him and made him choke? Well, Jim implied that you did the same thing to him," Janessa explained.

"Musta been something he ate," I said.

I'd pretended to brush Janessa's news aside. But after hanging up the phone I sat there, puzzled. I'd often felt alone since Basil left. Now I remembered something he'd told me once when I was feeling blue. He'd said, "Things are never totally bad as long as you have a friend who cares. And you can always count on me for that."

I wondered again what had spooked Jim Argus—and just how much I had to thank Basil for that.

5 THAT NIGHT I dreamed about Basil. He was so real in the dream that when I awoke, I felt like I'd lost him all over again.

The day only got worse as it went on. Dennie Plover and his brother Keith stopped at the gas station that afternoon.

"Isn't it nice to see there's a job for everybody? No matter how serious the handicap?" Dennie taunted.

"Pay for your gas and get lost," I said.

"Let's see," Dennie drawled, "How much do I owe?"

"$7.60," I said, ignoring his smirk.

Dennie turned to Keith. "You got any money?"

"Yeah," Keith said, spilling coins from his pockets. They were mostly pennies, and they tumbled from the counter all over the floor.

"Uh-oh," Dennie said to me. "Looks like you've got a little mopping up to do."

"Pick them up, you clowns," I snapped.

"And you call this service?" Dennie mocked.

I'd had enough. "Sal!" I yelled, and in two seconds my boss appeared. "Sal, these two very funny guys just threw the money they owe for gas on the floor. Now they don't want to pick it up."

A nasty smile crossed Sal's face. "Hey, my men, you scratch that money off the floor, okay? Especially you, Keith Plover. My cousin is your parole officer, and he wouldn't be too pleased about this," Sal said.

The Plovers gave Sal an evil look. But they bent down and began scooping up the coins. Sullenly they plunked them on the counter and stalked back to their car. As they roared off, they must have stripped a quarter inch of rubber off their tires.

Sal watched them take off, shaking his head. "What do they use for brains? And where do they get money for a set of wheels like that?"

Yeah, I just wonder, I thought grimly. By putting on ski masks and ripping off cabbies maybe? Neither Dennie nor his brother had any kind of job—yet they always seemed to have enough cash. Their parents weren't rich. Surely they weren't handing out enough money to keep up a black T-Bird—even an old one that needed washing.

When Gil came in for a cola, I shared my suspicions with him. "I bet the Plover brothers are ripping off the cabs, Gil."

Gil wiped his brow with the back of his sleeve. He'd been doing oil changes and tune-ups all morning. "I wouldn't be surprised, especially with Keith. He's a hard case. They bothering you, Val?"

"Just the usual," I said.

"You don't have to put up with stuff from them," Gil said.

"I don't want you getting involved, Gil. I can handle it myself," I said quickly. I was seeing the protective look on Gil's face a lot lately. I knew he cared about me. But I didn't want him getting hurt on my account.

"Word's been going around that Jim Argus is a little nervous lately," Gil said proudly.

"Yeah," I said. "Jim's always been a

coward though. The Plovers could be dangerous. I sure wish the police would check them out on this cab crime spree."

"You really think the Plovers are the ones doing the crimes, Valerie?" Gil asked.

"It's just a hunch, Gil," I admitted.

"Well, you're pretty smart. Man, I remember in school how you'd ace all the exams. If you figure it's the Plovers doing the crimes, you're probably right."

When I got home from work, Dad was in really high spirits. "I sold two cars!" he bellowed, beating his chest proudly in mock self-pride. "Mr. Everly said I'm doing better than the young guys. Do you realize what that does for the self-esteem of a guy with gray hair? And the money! I'll be taking home more this week than I did all month driving a cab!"

"That's fantastic!" I cheered "I always knew you were great. Now the world is finding out too."

"How about that? It takes a guy like me over thirty years to find my true calling—a salesman! All these years pushing a truck and here was this dynamite salesman inside me crying to get out and do his stuff!" Dad laughed.

For dinner that night Mom cooked the best steaks she could find, covered with a delicious mushroom sauce. As the three of us ate, we laughed and chatted. It was the best dinner the family had had in a long time.

"Just think of it," Mom said as we washed up after dinner. "Your father could still be driving that awful cab."

"Like that poor man who almost lost his eye," I said.

"Do you know that your history teacher at Hawthorne, Mr. Kramer, is driving a cab this summer?" Mom asked me.

"Mr. Kramer? You're kidding!" I gasped.

"I know it sounds crazy. But he's got four kids, and the teachers took a pay cut this year. He had to earn some extra money."

\* \* \*

On Sunday I kept my date with Gil and our friends. We all started talking about our plans for the fall—and then for the future.

As we talked, I felt a twinge of sadness for Mr. Kramer and all the poor cabbies out there that night. I was so grateful that my dad wasn't one of them.

I asked Gil what he wanted to do with his life. It's funny, but I always thought he was just a jock with no interests beyond football. I'd never thought of him as a good student. Well, maybe I'm prejudiced like everybody else. Like Mrs. Gottsman had told us, "Prejudice is a tricky thing— sometimes it hides so cleverly, you don't even see it in yourselves." So I guess I was prejudiced against jocks! This was a part of me I'd never really been aware of.

In reply to my question, Gil said, "Well, I'm interested in fossils."

Janessa burst out laughing. "You don't even know what a fossil is, Gil! Get real!"

Janessa's boyfriend laughed too. "Come on, man. We know you from way back."

Gil didn't get mad, but I'd never seen him look so hurt before. It was as if some-body had slapped him across the face. A lot of guys would have given back in kind, or responded with some choice insults. But Gil was quiet and dignified. I admired him for that.

"Remember when we were all in junior

high and that professor came and talked about fossils?" Gil ventured.

"Yeah. *She* was a fossil herself," Tom sneered.

"That joke is a fossil!" I shot back. Then I fixed my gaze on Gil. "I remember her. She was trying to talk kids into going to Colorado to dig for dinosaur bones or something. I thought it was a pretty cool idea, but it was expensive."

"Yeah," Gil said with a big smile, "Man, here I was, a thirteen-year-old kid who didn't care about anything but football—and I was excited. Well, I told my folks I wanted to go. But they couldn't pay. So down at the church they took up a collection for me to go. Can you beat that? Me, a budding paleontologist."

"You actually went?" I asked him. Why didn't I remember something like that? Because I never paid any attention to Gil, that's why. I always felt kind of superior to guys like Gil. My friends and I were cool and smart and jocks were, well, *dummies.*

"Yeah, I went to the Snake Valley Research Preserve. We walked for almost two miles, and there they were...real dinosaur bones!" Gil's face lit up like a Christmas tree. I had to smile too. I was both surprised and delighted to see this side of Gil.

"For three days we dug. We found fossilized roots of cattails and fish skeletons. And we worked with paintbrushes, whisk brooms, and even little dental picks and plastic straws. Man, I was so proud of my tool kit. I can still remember taking pictures of that place, talking to the other kids there, sharing what we found. You guys are gonna think I'm crazy to say this, but it was more fun than any touchdown I ever made on the football field. It was great to do something worthwhile. Something that would mean more than a great catch."

Everybody, even Dina's and Janessa's boyfriends, were quiet now, staring at Gil and kind of nodding.

"Yeah," Tom said, "I know what you mean. It'd be great to be...well, not famous. Maybe just a name in an index somewhere," he said with a laugh.

"You really gonna be a...what did you call it?" Wallie asked.

"Paleontologist," Gil said. "Yeah, I am. It might take me a while, but that's what I'd like to end up doing."

I just sort of stared at Gil and realized how stupid I'd been all this time.

**6** THAT NIGHT WHEN I got home, my mom asked me how my date had gone.

"Mom, you'd be amazed at what a cool guy Gil really is. I mean, he's into digging for dinosaur bones. We're going to a museum, and he's going to take me on a tour of the fossil section."

"This is getting to sound serious," Mom said. "I mean, when a couple digs bones together, anything can happen."

"Right, Mom," I laughed. "It's just that I always thought Gil was...uh...well, you know, he played football and..." I trailed off, my face turning warm.

"A dumb jock, I know," Mom laughed. "Well, I'm glad you've dug deeper and discovered differently. And I'm glad I can trust you to pick good friends." She sighed and shook her head. "Thank God, I'm not Jan Draper's mother."

"What do you mean?" I asked.

"I ran into Jan's mother the other day.

She's really worried about her daughter. Jan hangs around with Dennie Plover all the time, and Mrs. Draper hates that."

Thinking of Jan made me shudder. I remembered that terrible trick she'd played on our teacher Mrs. Gottsman during our senior year. Mrs. Gottsman had survived a Nazi concentration camp. Jan had rigged it so there were Nazi swastikas all over the walls and Hitler's shrieking voice blaring over a record. Mrs. Gottsman was so upset that she had to be hospitalized.

"I don't know what Jan ever saw in Dennie," I said.

"Whatever it is, it hasn't done her any good. Mrs. Draper said you wouldn't recognize Jan. She doesn't take care of herself. She smokes and drinks and just lies around all day like a zombie," Mom said. "And she'd do anything for Dennie. She's like a puppet and he pulls the strings."

"She's always been like that where Dennie's concerned. I remember he gave her some junk jewelry for playing that awful trick on Mrs. Gottsman. Jan acted like it was buried treasure," I said.

I had Monday off, so Gil called me at home that night. After telling me about his day, he fell silent for a moment. "Say, Valerie, I've got something to tell you...I went to the police today."

"What!"

"Listen, don't get mad. I know how you feel about accusing people. But I think there's good grounds to suspect the Plovers. When innocent lives are at stake, you can't keep your suspicions to yourself."

My thoughts spun in a whirlwind. Was Gil right? Should I have gone to the police myself? And what would happen now? I hoped that it would never get back to the Plovers that Gil had set the police on their trail.

"Don't worry about it, Valerie. Lt. Hardy said he'd be real cool about looking into it. He promised not to mention my name," Gil said.

"I hate to think what Dennie and his brother might do if they found out you tipped the police," I said.

"Look, I didn't tell anybody but Lt. Hardy...except for you and my family," Gil said.

"Your family...Isn't your sister a sixth-grader at King Elementary?" I asked him.

"Yeah...so?" Gil asked.

"You don't think Monique will say anything, do you? Dennie's girlfriend, Jan Draper, has a sister at King too," I said.

There was a pause. "I don't think Monique was even listening when I was telling my parents about calling the police. But anyway, I'll warn Monique not to say anything."

I said goodnight to Gil, but I was worried sick. I remembered too well being Monique's age. Secrets never lasted long. Even in summer, when school was out, kids always ran into each other at places like the beach or the mall.

I tried to calm myself. Monique and Jan Draper's sister probably weren't even friends. And so what if Gil called the police about something? It was unlikely Monique would even mention something like that to her friends. Wasn't it?

The next day at work, I couldn't help but bring up the subject again. Gil tried to reassure me. "If the Plovers aren't guilty of hitting those cabs, then they've got no reason to fear the police investigating them. If they're the ones responsible, well then I did the right thing. I have no regrets."

Something in Gil's voice made me ask, "Gil, is there anything wrong?"

He shrugged slowly and looked sheepish. "Well, it seems like Monique has a big, big mouth. She was with a group of her friends, and someone mentioned Dennie Plover for some reason or other. So of course, Monique had to get in on the conversation and bring up my call to the police. Well, Kira Draper happened to be there."

"Oh, Gil, no!" I groaned.

"It's my fault," Gil said. "I sorta forgot what an eleven-year-old kid is like. I never should have spoken in front of Monique."

All during the day I was tense, waiting for the other shoe to drop. I figured Dennie and Keith were fighting mad by now. Who knew what they'd do?

I was especially worried about Gil—and in that sense the joke was on me. I had pretended to like Gil just to fool my parents. Well, now I not only really liked him, but I was beginning to care deeply about him. Every new thing I learned about Gil only increased my admiration and respect for him. And I liked the way he supported me and stood up for me. It terrified me to think of something happening to him.

Well, nothing happened for two days. I even allowed myself the stupid hope that Kira Draper, for some reason, hadn't told Jan. Maybe she hated her big sister or something. Then I figured maybe the police had cleared the Plovers, and the whole thing would pass. But I didn't really believe that—not for more than a few seconds.

Then on Wednesday, Gil's day off, Dennie Plover showed up at the gas station.

"Hey, Valerie," he snarled when he came in to pay for his gas. "What's up?" His face was expressionless, except for his eyes. He reminded me of a snake before it strikes.

"Nothing," I replied, making change from a twenty. Then I gripped the counter, trying to brace my nerves.

"Cops were nosing around our place.

They figured me and my brother were the ones hitting the cabbies," Dennie said. "How'd the cops get a crazy idea like that?" He paused, smiling faintly at me, enjoying my obvious discomfort. He loved to make people afraid.

"So what happened? Did they find anything?" I asked, trying to act indifferent.

Dennie smirked. His gaze bore into me like a drill. Then he laughed. He had a really hideous laugh—the kind you hear in horror movies when the mad scientist finally concocts the devilish potion.

"Get lost, Dennie. I've got to stock the racks," I said.

But Dennie stayed where he was. "I know who tipped the cops," he said.

I struggled to remain calm. "You act like I'm supposed to know what you're talking about," I said.

"Your voice is shaky, Valerie. Are your knees knocking too? I think I can hear them." He turned, held the door open, and whistled as if to call a dog. I followed his gaze and spotted Jan Draper emerging from Dennie's T-Bird. She strolled slowly into the office, a cigarette dangling from her lips. Wisps of hair dangled in her face.

"Tell Valerie what your sister told you, Jan," Dennie said.

Valerie fixed her glassy stare on me and said, "Kira told me that Gil Sheffield called the cops. He gave them the hot tip that maybe Dennie and his brother've been robbing the cabs."

What could I say? "Kids get stories all mixed up," I protested weakly.

"Okay, get back in the car, Jan," Dennie said.

"Dennie, I'm starved. I want to buy some chips or something." Her gaze roamed the racks.

"Get back to the car," Dennie repeated, giving Jan a shove. With one sleepy gaze behind her, Jan obeyed him. Dennie returned his attention to me. He made a gun from his hand, aiming the index finger at me. "It's payback time," he said.

"You'd better watch yourself, Dennie. If you hurt anybody you'll be in bigger trouble than you've ever been before," I warned. I tried hard to make my voice sound braver than I really felt.

"You're hot for him, aren't you? You

really see something in that stupid football player, Sheffield. I like that. It makes
what I'm gonna do twice the fun," Dennie
said. "Payback time. You remember that.
Late at night when you wake up, remember—payback time."

Dennie turned and swaggered out. I felt
like I'd just been drenched by an ice-cold
rain shower. I called Gil immediately.

"He doesn't scare me," Gil said when I
told him.

"Maybe he should," I replied. I remembered Dennie and Keith coming at Basil
with tire chains, blood in their eyes.

"Listen, Val, I remember when Dennie
didn't make the football team at
Hawthorne. I can still see him whining
and crying about it. He made some big-
time threats against me then 'cause I was
the team captain. One afternoon it was
him and me in the gym. He was cryin' for
mercy in two seconds. I don't worry about
roaches like the Plovers."

I recalled that when Basil Harris con-
fronted the Plovers, I'd been scared too.
However, there was one difference—Basil
was indestructible. Gil Sheffield wasn't.

When the Plovers smashed the chains into Basil's face, the wounds had mysteriously vanished. I was kidding myself if I thought the same thing would happen to Gil. If they beat Gil like that, his life could be in danger. The thought scared me more than anything ever had before.

Nothing happened Wednesday. I heard from Dina that her uncle—who was on the police force—told her they'd found no solid evidence linking the Plovers to the cab robberies. Maybe Dennie and Keith were guilty as sin, but the police had nothing to hang a case on. So they were free to roam the streets...until they did something and got caught.

On Thursday night around six, the phone rang in our house. I don't know why, but I stared at it a long time before I answered it. Somehow I knew it was bad news—and I didn't want to hear it.

Finally I picked up the receiver. On the other end a woman's voice sobbed, "Valerie, this is Mrs. Sheffield, Gil's mother. Gil asked me to call you. He's been arrested! They're saying he's the one who's been robbing those cabbies!"

7 "HOW COULD THEY think that?" I almost screamed into the phone. Gil and his family were good, decent people. How could the police think Gil would be robbing cab drivers?

Mrs. Sheffield continued. Her voice sounded like a flute out of whack. "They came in here and said a witness identified my son as the robber. And then they took my boy away!"

"What witness?" I asked.

"They wouldn't say. They don't tell you anything. They never do. Why should they care?" Mrs. Sheffield sounded as if she might start sobbing again.

My dad saw how upset I was, and he took the phone from me. He listened for a minute, then asked, "Do you have a lawyer, Mrs. Sheffield?" Obviously she didn't, so Dad said, "It just so happens I sold a car to a very nice young attorney. Let me call her and see if she can help you out. This seems to me to be a clear case of mistaken identity. Now you just take it easy, Mrs. Sheffield. I'll call the lawyer and get back to you."

When my father put down the phone, I sank down to a chair in shock. "Oh, Dad, how could this be happening? I bet Dennie Plover got somebody to lie just to get Gil in trouble!"

"Very possible, I'm afraid. It's ridiculous to think a boy like Gil could commit crimes like that. This'll all be straightened out in short order. If Plover rigged some phony witness, it won't hold water. Gil will be free in the morning." My father kissed my brow and called the lawyer, Yoriko Miki.

After listening to my father, Ms. Miki agreed to meet us at the Sheffields' home after she had been to the police station. It was late in the evening when she finally arrived at the Sheffields', where my father and I were waiting with Mrs. Sheffield and Monique. I was surprised at how young Ms. Miki was. She couldn't have been more than twenty-seven or so. But it was obvious from the start that Ms. Miki was a very dedicated professional.

"I've spoken to both your son and the police," Ms. Miki began. "Unfortunately, bail is going to be a problem. Since these cab robberies were so violent and brutal, and one man stands to be permanently impaired, the bail will be very high. I'm not sure we can get Gil out as quickly as I'd hoped."

"Who is this witness the police talked about?" Mrs. Sheffield asked.

"A girl he went to school with—Jan Draper. She claims she saw him remove the ski mask in an alley just after the last robbery," Ms. Miki said.

"She's Dennie Plover's girlfriend," I cried. "She'd lie for him in a minute!"

"Yes," Ms. Miki said, "and we'll bring that out at the hearing. It's obviously a frame-up. If that's all the evidence they have, we'll be all right."

"What other evidence could they have?" Mrs. Sheffield protested. "He's innocent!"

"Well, the Draper girl said she followed Gil. She claimed she watched him stash something in a shed behind the gas station where he works. So the police have gone there," Ms. Miki reported.

"Anybody could go into that shed," I said. "It's never locked."

"I'm sure your son will be cleared quickly, Mrs. Sheffield," Ms. Miki said. "Please try not to worry. I'll be in touch the moment I hear anything." Then she picked up her briefcase and left.

Dad and I drove home past the gas station where Gil and I worked. The police were there talking to Sal and checking the shed. "This is Dennie's way of getting even with Gil," I said to my father. "You know, the kids said that Basil had special powers to make horrible things happen to bad people. I wish I could cast a spell on Dennie Plover to make him tell the truth."

"It'll be okay, honey. Yoriko Miki is a sharp lawyer," Dad said. "She'll blow away all the nonsense."

It turned out that the police did find a ski mask in the shed. But they didn't find any cash or jewelry from the robberies.

After two days, Gil's bail was lowered, and his mother and grandfather were able to get the money together. We were all waiting for him as he came out. His mom, Monique, and I all hugged him.

"Oh, honey," his mother sobbed.

"It'll be okay, Mom," Gil said. "When I get my hearing, they'll see through the frame."

"Dennie did it," I said grimly. "He just as good as told me he would. He called it 'payback time.' He got that fool Jan to lie for him and they stashed some stupid ski mask in the shed. Now I'm more sure than ever that they're the ones who've been robbing the cabbies. If only we could prove it and get those creeps nailed!"

"Take it easy," Gil said softly. I couldn't believe how calm he was after being in jail for something he never did. It was so unfair, so incredibly unfair.

"You've got to be careful, Gil," his mother said. "You've always been a good boy. But for heaven's sake, now is not the time to give them a reason to suspect you of *anything.*

"Nobody in our family ever was in trouble with the law," Mrs. Sheffield went on. "I could have died when they came and took you away."

The next day Gil and I went for burgers at a place next to the doughnut shop. I just wanted some time alone with him.

"I bet it was awful down there in jail, huh, Gil?" I asked him.

"Pretty awful. The worst part is the humiliation. Knowing you didn't do anything and yet being treated like a criminal," he said.

"It breaks my heart that this happened, Gil," I said. "I feel like it's all my fault."

"It's not your fault at all. I'm the one who called the police about the Plovers. Listen, don't worry. It's gonna be okay. Ms. Miki says so. But it's scary how quick you can lose it all. How one minute you're free and the next they're taking your fingerprints. I do wonder what other evidence Dennie Plover might've planted to make me look guilty. And if it is the Plovers and they hit another cab, am I gonna get blamed for that too?"

"You've got to be really careful," I told him. "Always make sure people know where you are in case something else does happen."

We both went back to work at the gas station. Sal was really sympathetic. "You got framed, kid. It happens," he said, clapping Gil on the back.

Things were quiet for the next couple of days. But one night, just before I was about to go to bed, the frantic sounds of sirens filled the air. I always hate those sounds because it means tragedy for somebody. But now I was especially on edge. I turned on the radio for the local news. There was a talk show on, and two men were screaming at each other about gun control. I thought it would never end. But finally the announcer came on with a local update.

"Another in a series of vicious cab attacks has taken place tonight on Grand Avenue," the news reporter said in her crisp, unemotional voice. "During an attempted robbery, a cab driver was attacked and struck on the head with a blunt object. Police are not yet identifying the driver, who is reported to be in critical condition at this hour. One witness described the attacker as a burly man wearing a ski mask. A massive police search continues at this hour for the suspect, who fled after the attack."

I couldn't help worrying about Gil. I

knew he'd gone to a baseball game that night. What if he was driving home alone at the time of the robbery? What if he had no alibi for when it happened?

I wanted desperately to call Gil's house to see if he was home. But I didn't want to worry his mom. So I lay in bed and tried to sleep. Finally I couldn't stand it any longer. I switched on a lamp and dialed the Sheffields' number.

"Mrs. Sheffield, it's Valerie," I cried into the phone. "Is Gil home?"

"No," she said. "And I just heard that another cabbie was robbed right down the street! Where can Gil be?!"

"I'm sure he'll be home any minute," I said.

After I hung up, I walked over to my rose petal and lifted the glass lid. The sweet scent surrounded me as it always did. But this time something was wrong, and I began to cry. My heart was breaking, and I didn't know what to do.

8 IT WAS MY mother who told me the awful news the next morning. The cab driver who'd been attacked the night before had died—and it was Mr. Kramer, our history teacher! At first, I was too stunned to react to the news. Then I cried until my eyes ached.

And as if things weren't already bad enough, Gil had never gone home. He'd called his mom and said he was afraid the cops would nail him again if he turned up. He was scared he'd be blamed for Mr. Kramer's murder. He'd told his mother to tell me he was sorry.

I kept remembering all those classes when Mr. Kramer had breathed some life into the usual dry history lectures. He'd made learning history fun. I couldn't imagine even Dennie Plover being low enough to kill Mr. Kramer. And what would become of his wife and four kids?

In mid-morning Dina and Janessa and I got some baskets of groceries and flowers and a special letter together. We wrote how much we all respected Mr. Kramer. Then we walked over to the Kramer house.

On the way over, I told Dina and Janessa about Gil.

"Mrs. Sheffield thinks he's hiding out in the neighborhood," I said. "He's terrified somebody is gonna try to pin the murder on him."

"How could any fool think Gil could be a murderer!" Dina said.

"Yeah," Janessa said. "That guy has the biggest heart in the world."

"They oughta be arresting the Plovers," Dina said.

"One witness last night said the guy in the ski mask was big and muscular," Janessa said. "Dennie is kinda skinny and not very tall."

"Keith is big," I pointed out. "And he's been convicted of a robbery already. He's on parole."

"I'd just like to get as far from this place as I could," Janessa said. "Valerie, you're a fool not to grab that scholarship to Iowa and stay there. I hear there's hardly any crime in the Midwest. I'd rather live there than here where a poor history teacher gets killed driving a cab!"

"I'm sure things like this happen even in the Midwest," I said. "Besides, most people who live here are good. And we get along. There are lots of different kinds of people, but we all get along. Why should a few evil creeps drive us out?"

"I just dread seeing Mrs. Kramer," Janessa said. "Imagine how she's feeling."

"Yeah," Dina agreed. "Maybe we shouldn't even be doing this. Maybe we'll just cause her pain."

"No," I said. "She's got four kids. Four little kids. With all the stuff Mrs. Kramer has to deal with, she'll be glad she won't have to bother about meals."

"Look," Janessa said softly, "there's the house. Remember when Mr. Kramer had us all over to practice for the multicultural celebration we did at the assembly?"

I swallowed hard and forced back the tears. The last thing Mrs. Kramer needed was to face the three of us, dripping with tears.

"Maybe we should just leave the stuff on the porch, " Dina suggested.

"No," I said. "We should check to see if Mrs. Kramer needs anything else."

We went up the three steps to the porch. There were flowers and shrubs around the house and a little vegetable garden in the side yard. You could tell a nice family lived there.

I touched the doorbell. Almost immediately a woman answered the door. She was an older woman—older than I'd pictured Mrs. Kramer.

"Hello," I said to her, "we came to see Mrs. Kramer. We used to be students of Mr. Kramer, and we're so sorry about what happened to him. We've brought Mrs. Kramer something to help her out a little." We held out our baskets of groceries and flowers.

"Oh, how thoughtful," the woman said, smiling. "I'm Mrs. Cerillo, a friend of the family. I'm afraid Mrs. Kramer isn't really up to seeing visitors just now. But I'll be glad to take those from you and see that she gets them." She took the baskets and set them inside the door.

"Of course, we understand," I said. "We wrote a letter too, about uh...about how much he meant to all the kids. It's in one of the baskets." I couldn't stop the tears anymore. They ran down my face. I saw that Dina and Janessa were crying too. I knew we had to leave before we broke down completely. I said to Mrs. Cerillo, "Please tell Mrs. Kramer we're so sorry."

"I surely will," she replied with another kind smile. Then she shut the door.

As I walked Dina and Janessa home, we passed the doughnut shop. I glanced in and saw Mrs. Dowd at the counter. Usually she looked so prim and neat. But now her hair was all unruly, like she hadn't even bothered to comb it this morning. I figured she was missing my efficiency. Even her grouchy son said I did the work of three people. But I was too heartsick to gloat about Mrs. Dowd getting her just dues for firing me. I was crushed by Mr. Kramer's death and worried sick about Gil.

Later in the day I found out that the police had told Gil's mother that they wanted to talk to Gil. They said he'd better turn himself in. Ms. Miki, the lawyer, was also anxious for Gil to appear. She knew that his hiding out didn't look very good for her client.

"Dennie and Keith have alibis," Dina told me.

"They're good at getting people to lie for them," I said bitterly.

"It looks really bad for Gil to be hiding out like this," Dina said. "It makes him seem guilty."

I turned sharply. "Dina, you said yourself that only a fool would suspect Gil!"

"Yeah, I know," Dina said nervously. "But I was talking to my uncle. Remember, I told you about my uncle who's a cop on the East Side? Anyway, he said if you *act* guilty, a judge and jury will usually assume you *are* guilty."

I walked home from Dina's house feeling worse than ever. As I passed the gas station, I decided to call and ask Sal for the day off. I couldn't bear to work there that day. When I passed the doughnut shop again, Mrs. Dowd was still rushing around like crazy. She looked really unhappy. I figured she was feeling sorry for herself over having so much work, but she didn't know what real trouble was. Real trouble was being Mrs. Kramer, a widow with four little kids. All Mrs. Dowd had to worry about was a lazy son like Rick.

I couldn't eat any dinner, even though Dad was trying to cheer me up with tales of all his funny customers. He told of one guy from Kuwait who wanted to buy three new cars, one for each son. And the sons couldn't even drive yet!

Suddenly, Dad stopped talking about his customers. He glanced at Mom and then said to me, "Honey, I think you should go to Iowa after all and use that scholarship. The family finances are really looking up now. It won't be any strain on us."

"Yes," my mother chimed in, "especially since what's happened with Gil."

I stared at my mother. "What's happened with Gil? Some hoods framed him for those robberies, and now he's scared they'll frame him for murder too. What's happened hasn't changed my feelings for Gil," I said.

"Darling," my mother said, "you know the main reason you were staying home was because you were worried that your dad and I couldn't cover your college expenses. Gil was an afterthought."

"Maybe in the beginning," I said. "But now I really care about Gil."

Mom reached over and touched my arm. "Valerie, I know you don't want me to say this, but have you given any thought to the possibility that Gil could be involved in those crimes?"

"Mom!" I stared at her in shock.

"Wait a minute, Valerie," my mother said. "I'm not saying he committed the actual robberies. But what if he's been an accomplice? Maybe Gil fell in with an older guy—someone who offered him some easy money. You know Gil's family has never had a lot of money."

I didn't wait to hear another word. I tore away from the table and ran to my room, slamming the door behind me. Tears were streaming down my cheeks. A horrible, nagging fear was in me, growing like a scrub fire. The reason Mom's words set me afire was that I'd thought the same dark thoughts.

Gil had hung out sometimes in high school with guys who were trouble-makers. He'd never been able to turn his back on an old friend. Once he had said to me, "Valerie, what if all the clean guys turned against the troublemakers? Then the troublemakers would have nobody but other troublemakers for friends. And they'd probably never straighten out."

But no way in the world could Gil ever get mixed up in crimes. Never!

For hours I battled my worries and sorrow over Mr. Kramer and Gil. Finally, sometime after midnight, I fell asleep from sheer exhaustion. But it wasn't a restful sleep. I had nightmares of Gil being cornered by the police in some empty warehouse. Over and over I saw Gil run and the cops draw their guns. Then, suddenly, I was standing before the bronze statue of William Evans Hawthorne in the schoolyard. The sun was shining, and I felt a warm hand grasp mine.

"Basil!" I gasped.

"Valerie, you're crying," he said. He wore a blue checkered shirt and jeans. He opened his arms, and I took shelter in them. "You're trembling too."

I felt his strong hands on my back. For the first time in many days I felt comforted.

9 "BASIL, MR. KRAMER, our history teacher, was murdered. And they're blaming Gil Sheffield. You remember Gil, don't you?"

"Sure. He won a couple of big games for Hawthorne. A really nice guy. Like a little boy in a man's body, all full of happiness and enthusiasm," Basil said.

"He's innocent, Basil," I whispered. "Gil could never hurt anybody!"

"Of course not," Basil said.

"But he's hiding. I'm so scared that he'll do something stupid if the police corner him and he'll get hurt trying to run away."

Basil put the back of his hand on my cheek, wiping off the tears. "It'll be all right, Valerie. Now listen closely: There's a storage rental place on Grand—28D."

"What?" I asked.

"Valerie, I love you, and I always will," Basil said.

"Basil!" I cried out in the darkness when I couldn't feel his warmth anymore. "Basil!"

The next moment, my father was shaking me gently. "Valerie, wake up, honey. You're having a nightmare."

"No," I said, "it wasn't a nightmare. It couldn't have been—it was too real to have been a dream, Dad."

"Some of them can be. I remember after my grandfather died. I was about eleven at the time. He and I used to go fishing all the time, and hiking—just hanging out. Well, after he died, I dreamed of him night after night. Then, one night there was this very real dream. My grandfather said to me, 'Boy, it's been grand, but it's time we both moved on.' And that was the last of the dreams. By heaven, they were real!"

I nodded slowly.

"You okay now, sweetheart?" Dad asked, kissing my brow.

"Fine, Dad," I said. As he was going out the door, I asked him, "You know that Gil is innocent, don't you, Dad?"

"Sure thing," he said, giving me a wink. It was our private signal to remind each other that we were in agreement. "And everybody will know he's innocent before long, honey."

In the morning I begged off work again. "I've got something really important to do, Sal," I explained. Then I got together with Dina and Janessa at Janessa's house.

"I had this, uh, dream that there's something important at that storage rental place on Grand—in 28D," I told them.

Dina and Janessa looked at me as if I'd flipped my lid. "What are you talking about?" Janessa asked.

"Well, it wasn't exactly a dream. I sorta saw Basil and he told me," I said.

Dina's eyes got very big. "Basil Harris? Val, are you saying *you saw him?*"

"Yeah, in a dream, but it wasn't a dream. Oh guys, please don't make me try to explain it because I can't! But we've got to watch that storage place because I think the guy who's doing these cabbie crimes stashed his stuff there."

"If you really think that's true, don't you think we should tell the police?" Dina asked.

"No. I mean, you guys might play along with me. But do you think the cops would? They'd just think that Gil had told me where *he* put the loot," I said.

"Hey," Janessa said, "my grandma stores some of her stuff in that place. There's an old warehouse with lots of busted windows on the corner. My brother and his friends play in there. You can look down from the warehouse's second floor and see the rental storage yard. If we had binoculars, we could pick out 28D real easy..."

My heart began to race. Basil wouldn't have told me about 28D if it weren't crucial. "Janessa, I've got binoculars! We could take turns watching the place."

"But he probably only goes there at night," Dina protested. "Surely you don't mean..."

"No way am I playing detective in that place at night," Janessa said with a shiver.

"Okay, I'll do it myself," I said. "I'll cover with my parents by saying that I'm staying over at one of you guys' houses."

Dina and Janessa looked at each other helplessly.

"Oh shoot," Janessa groaned, "we can't let you go there all by yourself. We'll all go. Anyway, we've probably done stupider things than this. Though I can't exactly remember when."

I looked at Dina expectantly.

"Oh, fine, count me in," she said. I smiled gratefully at my two friends. Then we began an impatient countdown toward darkness. I called and told my parents we were having sort of a slumber party at Dina's house. I hated lying to them, but they'd never allow me to go snooping around in the middle of the night. And something deep inside me convinced me that we'd see Mr. Kramer's killer near 28D tonight.

When it was completely dark, we walked to the warehouse. The doors hung loosely on their hinges and swung back and forth in the wind. People who had no other place to stay often slept in the warehouse. Tonight we had to step over an old man snoring like a foghorn. Nobody bothered us as we went up the stairs to the second floor and crept to the window.

"Wow," I gasped, looking through the binoculars. "You were right, Janessa. I can see locker 28D really well. The yard is pretty well lit too. I guess it would help stop break-ins."

"Yeah," Janessa said, "they have a watchman too. But he's usually sleeping in the office. Grandma came one night to get some extra china for a big dinner, and she couldn't rouse the guy."

"So," Dina said, "let's get our act together, you guys. What if we see some creep going in 28D? What do we do?"

"I run downstairs as fast as I can over to the liquor store. Then I call the police from the pay phone," I said.

"What if it's Gil?" Dina asked.

"I could strangle you for saying that, Dina," I said.

"I'm risking my life for you, girl, and you want to strangle me? I'm just saying we've got to prepare for anything," Dina said.

"Well, it won't be Gil," I said.

Janessa had brought along a bag of chocolate chip cookies and some cans of cola. "No use being hungry and thirsty while we wait," she said.

We kept watch in the warehouse until 12:30 in the morning. I was starting to think maybe I had imagined the whole dream. Maybe the number 28D was my old junior high gym locker and somehow it got all jumbled up with Basil's memory.

"Val!" Janessa grabbed my arm so hard, I almost cried out in pain. "See that guy over there? The big, burly guy in the over-coat—*in this weather!*"

I peered hard through the binoculars. "I can't recognize him with that cap pulled down over half his face!"

"He's heading for 28D all right," Janessa said.

"Can you recognize him?" I passed the binoculars to Dina.

"It could be any one of two dozen guys I know! Why doesn't the fool turn this way?" Dina groaned.

"He's at 28D," I gasped, putting down the binoculars. "Keep watching, you guys. I'm going down to call the police!"

"He's unloading stuff from a bag and putting it inside," Dina said. "Hurry up, Val!"

I sprinted out the door and ran down the stairs. Then, as I got to the bottom, two men blocked my path.

"Hey, baby, what's your hurry?" asked a tall, skinny man.

"Please, I've got to make an important

phone call," I cried, trying to get around them. The short one was wearing a black tank top and stocking cap. He laughed and blocked my way.

"Come on, honey. Don't ya wanna play?" the short one said.

"Will you please get out of my way? Somebody's life might depend on this phone call!" I yelled.

The skinny one put a hand on either side of the stairwell, cutting me off. "Look, we're not poison, hear what I'm saying? We're nice guys. Why don't you have some fun with us?"

I thought fast. Arguing with them was getting me nowhere. "Okay. Just let me make my phone call and I'll be back. Please!"

I don't know why—maybe it was even Basil's intervention—but they finally cleared a path for me. I raced past and reached the street, running toward the empty phone booth. I hoped I hadn't been delayed so long that the guy at 28D had left.

I dove into the phone booth. As I started to dial, a sharp voice said, "Put it down." I glanced behind me and saw the burly man in the ski mask standing at my shoulder. I was terrified—I thought my pounding heart would explode.

"I'm just calling my mom," I gasped, but I could tell he wasn't fooled. He aimed his gun right at me.

"Come out of there," he demanded. His voice sounded familiar, but I was too frightened to place it. I hung up the phone and came out slowly. I looked around, desperately hoping that there would be *somebody* on the street to help me.

He grabbed my arm and it felt like I'd been grasped by a pincer. Then with a quick glance around, he marched me down the silent street into an alley, where a dark car was parked.

"Please—I don't know you—just leave me alone," I stammered.

"You know me," he said.

"I don't!"

He jerked off the ski mask, and my heart jumped into my throat. "Oh no," I breathed.

"You knew me all the time from my voice, Valerie!" he snarled. "Don't try to play games with me. Now get in the car and drive!"

# 10

"RICK DOWD!" I finally gasped in disbelief. "*I—I can't drive!*"

He gave me a nasty shove that almost knocked me into the open door. "I've seen you drive, you little fool! Why are you out here spying on me anyway?"

I slid into the driver's seat and started the car. He sat beside me, the gun still pointed in my direction. Even now I couldn't believe that Rick Dowd was the one hitting the cabs, the one who killed Mr. Kramer.

"Stop looking at me like that," he said.

"But you—how could—"

He sneered. "Why not me? I'm twenty years old and I can't get a job that pays more than a few lousy bucks an hour. I have to work for my old lady—and if that isn't hell, I don't know what is. She's on my back twenty-four hours a day. Never gives me any peace. Calling me stupid and lazy, and makes me pay room and board to sleep in that rat hole. I end up without even enough to buy a pizza!

"So I started sneaking something out of the register now and then." He stopped and grinned at me.

"You...your mother fired me because she thought I was the thief!"

"Yeah. Ain't she wonderful?"

Just like her son, I thought grimly.

"But that was just pocket money," he went on. "It wasn't getting me anywhere. So I started pulling on a mask and making a couple hundred a night. So what?"

*But you killed Mr. Kramer,* I thought. *How could you have done that?* I was so shocked that I couldn't even form the words to ask.

"I'm a murderer, yeah," he said, as if reading my mind. "That wasn't my fault, you know? That idiot Kramer fought for his lousy money. He could be alive and kicking right now. But he fought for his pathetic ninety-eight dollars. He died for ninety-eight bucks! Most of it wasn't even his own money.

"I guess he thought because he was a football coach he could fight me and win.

I sure didn't start it anyway. I only used the tire iron when he forced me to. I didn't plan it. It just happened."

Perspiration streamed down my body as I drove. I'd never been so scared in all my life. If Rick had been willing to kill Mr. Kramer, then he'd kill me too. I knew what he'd done. He'd shoot me and leave me dead in some alley.

"It's like war," he said. "These streets are a battleground. A couple hundred have died in this city just in the last couple of years, you know. Soldiers fighting for a little piece of the action. Some live and some die—and what's it matter? Death is just the price you pay for walking the streets. If you want to get anywhere, you can't stop for fools who get in your way."

*Just keep talking, you idiot,* I silently begged. *Keep talking and don't notice where I'm heading.*

I fixed my gaze on a big row of silvery garbage cans. Then I hit the accelerator so hard that the car lurched, throwing Rick off balance. As I crashed into the garbage cans, I threw open the car door, scrambled out, and ran for my life.

Rick was behind me in seconds, cursing me as he ran. He would've shot me in a minute, but that would have attracted the attention of people in the surrounding apartments. It was a warm night and windows were open. I thought of screaming for help, but the running was taking all my breath. When I opened my mouth, nothing came out.

He was gaining on me, and I tried to run faster. My heart was on fire, and I could hardly breathe. Suddenly he lunged at me, grabbed my legs and threw me down on the street. It knocked the wind out of me, and I hit my head on the ground. At last I gathered enough strength to scream, "Help! Help me!"

Rick scrambled on top of me, and reached for my throat. Dimly, I heard loud music from one of the apartments. I knew my screams blended in with all the other raucous night sounds. I tried to scratch at his eyes, but couldn't reach them. He was too strong. His eyes were savage and cold, as though any kind of human feelings had long since died in him.

I'd given up hope when out of the

darkness, another figure appeared. Somebody had heard my cries! The stranger bent down and dragged Rick away from me. They grappled on the street. As the stranger drew back his arm, I noticed the initials *B.H.* on his shirt.

I must have blacked out then. The last thing I saw was the two men pummeling each other.

I woke up on a cot in the emergency room of the hospital. My parents were there, and so were Dina and Janessa.

"Take it easy, honey," my father said, seeing the question in my eyes. "Everything's going to be all right. The police have arrested Rick Dowd. He was pretty well beaten by that good Samaritan who helped you. But he'll be ready to stand trial for murder and robbery in a few weeks."

"The police found most of the loot in that locker, Valerie," Janessa said. "So you were right on target."

"He confessed to everything," Dina said. "It's all over the news. They're saying some mystery man came by and helped you, Valerie, and then vanished. They're asking for him to come forward and get his proper recognition."

It came back to me then. The shirt with his initials *B.H.*—it was Basil Harris. I was as certain of that as I was my own name, but no one would believe me. There was really no point in even bringing it up. But as long as Basil and I knew the truth, it didn't seem to matter what others believed.

"You're going to be just fine, young lady," Doctor Landers told me. "You suffered a minor concussion and a few bruises where you hit the pavement. I don't see why you can't go home in the morning."

I thought of Gil then. "Gil! Has anybody told him?"

"I'm sure he must have heard the radio reports," Dina said. "That's all they're talking about."

A little while later the door opened, and Gil Sheffield stood there looking at me. "The police told me you were here, Val," he said softly.

"Oh, Gil," I cried.

He came over and bent down and

kissed me. He was holding something behind his back. He brought it around slowly, and placed it in my hand.

It was a lovely pink rose.

"Gil," I gasped, "where did you get this?"

"Some guy outside the hospital. He was just standing there. And when I passed him, he grabbed my arm and said, 'You're Gil Sheffield, aren't you? Well, give this to the girl you love and take care—both of you.' "

Gil shook his head. "I started to ask him his name, but he walked off before I could get the question out. Funny, though. He looked a little familiar." Gil squinted his eyes as if he were trying to place the stranger. Then he shrugged.

"It's my rose," I said. Somehow I knew it was the same rose that Basil had given me before—the one whose petal I kept in a glass dish at home. As I looked at the flower I found the spot where the petal had fallen off. I'll always believe it was Basil's last gift to me—a reminder that there was always a chance of something better as long as hope never died.